Chase the Dream

Nathalie M.L. Römer

ISBN-13: 9789188459381

Emerentsia Publications
Marielundsvägen 9c
711 95 Gusselby
Sweden
emerentsiabooks.com

Ordering Information:

Orders by U.S. trade bookstores and wholesalers. Please contact Ingram: One Ingram Blvd., La Vergne, TN 37086 • 615.793.5000 or visit www.ingramcontent.com.

Independently printed as a Swedish publication.

*This story has previously been appeared in the anthology **Rags to Riches: Cinderella Love Stories** which has since been discontinued.*

Interior design and layout by Emerentsia Publications.

Official Website:
nathaliemlromer.com

Official Facebook Page:
facebook.com/nathaliemlromer

Official Twitter Account:
twitter.com/nmlromer

Book website: nathaliemlromer.com/chase-the-dream

For my loving partner Anders.

Chapter 1

THE ECHO OF A LOUD engine echoes through empty offices. It causes Ella to jerk up from an exquisitely grandiose leather chair, which seems to retain its beauty despite old age. Ella had tiptoed upstairs from the cellars, after thinking that she's totally alone in the massive factory, that's supposedly devoid of any of the workers usually occupying it at this late hour of the day.

"Who's here still?"

Ella rushes through the room and stops abruptly at the door.

"Did the *bitch* come back for some after-hours work?"

Ella glances in both directions in the hallway.

"Who's out there?" Ella's voice echoes through the corridor.

"Only me, sweetheart. I'm the new cleaner."

Ella shrieks when a male voice calls out to her.

"No need to be afraid. I'm just here to clean up after the *bitch*, as you so kindly referred to her."

"Oops. You heard that?"

"Of course, sweetheart. I find it rather funny you call *her* that."

"Why?"

"Because you—and please don't feel offended by what

I'm telling you—but you're her step-daughter. I heard people talk about that, that's how I know. You're doing a job *here* that not many would do. You don't ever complain about it."

"I hate my job."

"So, do I, but I still do it."

"You could leave and get another job in a heartbeat."

"So, could you."

"No, I can't. She'd make certain no one will believe me when I say I worked here."

"Hmmm, if you say so, sweetheart."

"Stop calling me that."

"Fair enough."

"I'll just go *back* to what I was doing. Let's pretend *we* never met, okay. Please don't tell anyone I was here…"

"I won't."

Ella starts walking away, then walks back to the door, "Errr, can I know your name?"

"Max."

"Oh—right. Okay."

Ella walks away and sits down on the chair once more. She stares at the door from time to time frowning as it's obvious that the cleaner wants to make known he's still nearby. She hears him whistle the annoying song she'd heard a few times on the radio.

I wonder who he is. Why is he working this late? No one ever works this late.

Ella sighs, gets up and walks back to the door. She glances in the corridor and sees it empty. She takes off her shoes, and on her bare feet rushes through the corridor before the annoying cleaner is back.

Only a few minutes later, Ella stands leaning against the door of the small room that's *her* room in the factory. She stares at the long repair desk with all the products she still must test *that* evening. She knows that slacking isn't an option.

"Mother dearest will be so angry if I don't finish my work. But I guess I'll have to deal with that tomorrow."

Ella sits down on the small wooden chair. She picks up a bundle of something that should be a neat package of wires, but instead is a jumble that could easily be ball of wool that had been attacked by a playful cat.

"How the hell does this stuff get so messed up anyway?"

Deep down, Ella knows why the equipment is a mess. She'd seen one of her step-mother's most loyal employees cause the mess. It's obvious there were people in the factory buying favours from their boss, "I wish Dad was still here. He wouldn't have allowed *them* to behave in this way towards me, towards all the people here…"

Ella's head slumps down. She knows her situation is hopeless. *No one can save me from that bitch no matter what I do. I guess I'll have to throw in my lot with those here who are just as screwed over by the bitch as I am.*

Ella picks at the bundle in her hand. "Dammit, how am I ever going to fix this?"

"Want some help with that, sweetheart?"

"Oh my god, are you still here?" Ella shouts.

"Errr—yeah. I told you, my name. You never told me yours."

"Ella."

"Just Ella, or…?"

"Why do you want to know?"

"Can't a guy be curious? Like why you are here all alone when there's no one else here?"

"But you're here, so I'm not alone."

"If it was me here, I would have gone home hours ago. But something tells me it's better I stick around until after everyone has arrived. Something tells me that all these needs fixing before the *bitch* comes. Why do you call her that anyway?"

"Errr—no reason. But why would you help me?

"No reason, other than to be nice I guess."

"So, if you're doing this, then what do I do?"

"Take a nap, have something to eat. Do whatever you like—"

"I guess I could try your job and see if it's as boring as this."

"If you like. I'll make sure I'll have all this fixed by the time you're done playing with *my* gadgets."

"Sure. See ya later."

"See ya later, princess—Don't come back until it's midnight. Or you'll turn into a pumpkin when you enter this room."

"I'm certain you're too old to read fairy tales, but okay—"

Ella rushes off before Max can say anything further. She also rushes off because the comment, for reasons that are totally incomprehensible to her, had caused a bright red blush to appear on her face. And she doesn't want him to see it. She also feels her heart beating faster and not from the extra effort of walking fast.

It doesn't take long before Ella arrives at Max's gadgets. Though she grumbles under her breath when she sees it's a machine, and Ella feels a renewed disgust for anything mechanical. But just as she's about to turn, something on the gadget catches her attention. Someone meticulously had sanded off part of a name off the side of the machine. A letter 'C' is visible but looking closer she suddenly certain other letters were there in the past. Rust betrays that the vandalism had occurred years ago. Ella squints her eyes.

Hang on, does it say there what I think it says?

Chapter 2

Ella straightens up and glances around. She listens. In the distance, she can hear a rhythmic clunking sound and must guess that it's Max doing something to fix the equipment, "I guess he's having as much trouble sorting through it as I do. But I guess I can hold up my end of the deal and try to clean up."

She looks again at the 'gadget' wondering now why Max referenced it in such a manner. She sees a red knob and guesses it's the starter. She pushes it and jumps when the machine sputters to life though much louder than she'd anticipated.

"Is everything okay?"

Ella groans when she hears Max yell at the top of his lungs over the sound of the machine, "Yes, I'm fine, thanks." Ella yells back.

"Just sit down on top of the little stool. There are two handles. One for movement forward, one for the brush."

"I'll figure it out."

Ella looks at the roaring cleaner, *Yeah, I'll figure it out alright. Including why someone sanded off Dad's name. Could this be why 'Prince Max' was so keen on us swapping jobs? For me to see this…*

Ella smirks suddenly when she realises what Max had done. He'd offered her a way to undermine the bitch. She'd married her father, then when he died from a sudden heart attack, she'd somehow usurped the control of her father's company from his only daughter Ella. The bitch had brought her two daughters with her to help run the business, and slowly Ella saw her father's rather successful business fall to pieces right around her.

"I could have left with most of the others who left soon after that happened." Ella mumbles. "But I guess I stayed to protect the workers here. I guess I brought this on myself. I wish Dad was still *here*—"

Ella climbs on top of the cleaner. She looks down, "Okay, I can do this. One's for moving, the other for cleaning—Right. Okay, which one?"

She pushes against the left knob. She jerks forward then back when the cleaning machine comes to life.

"Ouch, I guess I need to be careful doing this."

Glancing around Ella spots the desks of her step-sisters, *no, better not do anything there because that will cause a lot of problems for Max. But it would be fun if I could do something.*

Ella is about to move on when she spots something strange on the desk. She climbs from the cleaning machine, and gingerly steps into the room. She walks to the desk where a single sheet of paper lies on the desk. Its position betrays that someone might have forgotten it. Ella frowns when she recognises a name on the bottom of the paper.

"What's anyone doing with Dad's paperwork? Who's using this?" Ella frowns angrily. She looks around the office that she knows, though vaguely, as used by one of her two step-sisters; both were given prominent roles in the company.

Ella looks through the glass partition at the cleaning machine, and stares once more at the place where someone had haphazardly sanded away the name that had been there, "The name *now* is 'C. Industries Inc'. It was 'Chase Industries' before. My Dad's name. *My* name…Does this mean that *they* stole all this from *me?*"

Ella walks out to the cleaning machine which makes a soft buzzing sound. She climbs on top of it. Sitting there silently, Ella stares aimlessly at the other end of the corridor. She knows that she just had to turn left there, and she'd be in front of one specific door: her step-mother's office door.

"Should I dare to go inside there and see what I can find there?" But Ella remains frozen in place on the cleaning machine. She's too afraid of the consequences. She shakes her head to dispel the fear that had now entered her mind. Ella's hand is on the handle to let the cleaning machine move forward when a soft pinging sound echoes through the corridor. She looks up and sees a light flicker up on the elevator display at the end of the corridor. She knows whose elevator it is. She glances behind her, then in a panic manages to steer the cleaning machine back around the corner where she'd come from minutes earlier. After climbing down, she quickly dashes forward and looks around the corner and sees her step-mother exit the elevator, obviously fluffing up her expensive coat in front of the mirror next to the elevator for her then to disappear towards her office.

"Won't be long before she'll come looking at my so-called progress—"

Ella turns and dashes to the stairs at high speed.

***

"**M**ax are you in here still?" Ella hisses under her breath while she glances towards the stairs, "Max?"

"Yeah, I'm almost done. Just *two* to go."

"I think we need to go back to our regular jobs. The bitch is here. If she sees you in here, I'll get a right old beating from her."

"Oh right. That's one good reason to stop what I'm doing. Let me explain quickly how to complete this task."

Ella sits down, for a moment wondering if the work ahead would be difficult or not.

"Just connect all these blue wires to these connectors that say 'A-D' next to them. The orange ones to the connectors that say 'R-D' next to them. Then you close this cover over them with these screws. They'll take the longest so do the wires on both first, then all the screws. You understand what to do?"

Ella nods, swallowing hard, then giggles.

"What's funny?"

"I don't think the guy who tells me what work to do knows how to do it. You make it sound so easy."

"I have a father who taught me electrical engineering since childhood. Though he chides me now for my current career choice."

"Cleaning?"

"After a fashion. But I better go because I can hear footsteps. You'll be okay alone with her?"

Ella nods, "I have to——"

Max leans forward, and he kisses Ella's forehead, "That's for courage." Max explains, winking at her.

Chapter 3

Ella feels her face. It feels hot. *Hopefully I'm not blushing. The bitch will wonder why. I can claim that it was hot here tonight.* She listens for the footsteps closing in. Listening to the sound the heels make on the concrete floor, Ella picks up the work still to do, then she mouths Max's instructions.

"Wipe that smirk off your face, Ella. I have investors coming in exactly twenty minutes. Make sure you're done with your work, or there will be consequences. They're here for the next three days. Spick and span—"

"I'm done in about five minutes."

"Don't take that tone with me, little girl."

"I'm *not* a little girl and—"

"When you talk like that you are. Just make sure you're *not* here when I'm back with the investors."

Ella just nods. She looks down, feeling her step-mother's eyes piercing through her like the laser cutters used in the room above her. She waits, then when she's met with silence, Ella glances up ever so slightly. The room is empty. She listens and hears the fading sound of the tap-tap-tap of fast-paced steps.

"Bitch." Ella whispers.

"I *agree*. Let me help *before* I go home."

"Hi Max." Ella sighs. "Did you hear all that?"

"I did. I guess I can help you every day, so *you* can avoid the 'consequences' she suggested."

"I know what it means. That means I'll be locked up for a day in there." Ella nods sideways. "That's my 'home'."

"She makes you sleep *here*?"

"I guess so. I can't do anything to stop her."

"Maybe I can help?"

"I doubt it. You better *go* before she sees you. If she sees you, you'll lose your job."

"There's other jobs. While I'll talk, I'll sort out these two items." Max points at the table.

"Not for me. And go ahead. You can do it so much faster than I can."

"Never say never. I will help you. Even if it's just to fulfil my father's wish for *me* to have a job as an electrical engineer, and it's used to help a damsel in distress."

"I'm not a—" Ella stops talking when a finger gently brushes over her cheek. She looks up. Max looks down at her. "Never say never." Max repeats softly. "I've been here long enough to have seen most of her behaviour. There's a way out for you. I will help you."

"This is the first time in fifteen years I feel hope."

"Good. Fifteen years?"

"Yes, that's how long ago my dad died."

"Roger Chase was your father?"

"Yes—How do you know his name?"

"I saw it on some papers in the bitch's office."

"Oh right."

"Okay, I've sorted this out. I'll go now. I think you have a minute left on the clock. See you tonight, okay."

Ella nods.

✱ ✱ ✱

Ella listens through the door to the murmur coming from the repair room. She hears several voices that sound foreign. Among the voices, she hears the annoying voices of her step-sisters., and then their bone-shattering giggle that seems to echo everywhere, even in her tiny room. She tries to make sense of what is said, but after some minutes of trying she must give up. It's clear that her step-mother, who gets everyone to call her Mrs Chase at events such as this, is the centre of attention in the group.

"Did I hear that right? She's taking credit for *my* work?" Ella frowns angrily, then pushes against the handle of the door. She pulls her hand away like she touched the piping hot side of a pan with food cooking over the stove. "Why is it locked? If they're talking about Dad's business I should be there. I'm *his* daughter. This is *my* inheritance. It's not hers. Now I know how Cinderella in the fairy tale feels when she's forbidden to go to the ball."

"Are you going mad in there?"

Ella scrambles onto her feet and backs away from the door. *Did she hear me? Did anyone else hear me?*

"Ellaaaaa, ooh Ellaaaa. Now, now, *little* girl. Mother says that *you* won't get out of there until tonight if you're crazy. Crazy girls don't come out."

You bitch. You're as much a bitch as your 'mother dearest'. Leave me alone already.

Ella looks behind her and, like many times before, she finds solace in the only thing of beauty in the moment. She feels the warmth of the sun caress her cheek as the sun rises. "I wish I was out there—" Ella whispers. "I wish I'd listened to Max and gone with him."

"Ellaaaa—" Ella glances back to the door. It seems the taunts coming from behind the door would continue for as long as the meeting is going on.

* * *

"Rapunzel, Rapunzel, let down your hair," a familiar voice whispers from behind the window. "Well, that's if I use a hair growth lotion, and grow my hair in five minutes and pull you up as you're down there and I'm up here."

"Max why are you here?" Ella whispers.

"I found some information."

"What information?"

"About your father. About Roger Chase. Is your real name Ellana Chase?"

"Errr—it is."

"You said that he's been gone for fifteen years."

"Yes, he died fifteen years ago."

"You were only eight years old when he died."

Ella nods, "I still miss him every day."

"I can't get you out of there right now, but I can make certain that the masquerade *stops* when the investors are gone. The law is on your side, and this all be over in three days. I'm on your side as well, just remember that."

Ella nods once more.

"I need to go now before they see me. Will you be, okay?"

"For the most part. Just that my step-sisters see me as some sort of perverted form of entertainment. They've been calling my name for the last fifteen minutes. But I guess I can live with it for three more days."

"Okay, I'll come check up on you as often as I can."

Ella hears fast footsteps fade into the distance. She looks out of the window and glances at few details of the

15

city beyond that she can see, which is now bathed in the orange hue of a rising sun.

Dad, I know you're somewhere out there. I miss you so much. Dad, guide Max to a way to help me…Please…

Chapter 4

ELLA WALKS SLOWLY TO THE door when the taunts stop and two pairs of footsteps rush away from it. Ella puts her ear to the door to listen. Silence…

I guess they all left for food.

Ella turns and walks to her bed. She sits down and stares at the floor. "I guess 'day one' starts whenever she opens the door. I wonder when Max plans to be back…if he'll come back at all—" She stops her monologue when familiar footsteps approach the door. She stares at the door, willing it to open without the presence of the 'bitch' outside it.

"Come outside."

"Okay, okay, I'm coming."

"Keep *that* tone to yourself. I have extra work for *you* to complete."

Ella waits until she's past her step-mother before rolling her eyes, but she says nothing remembering Max's words from minutes earlier.

"The investors want to see the rest of the factory. It needs to be clean today. But as you see the rest of the lazy employees want their weekend off. I guess that leaves only *you* to do this work."

Ella freezes in place, *Am I some sort of slave in her eyes? Is that what Max meant when he said he's working on getting me out of here?"*

"As I can divert their attention for so long, I suggest you get on with it. Spick and span."

Ella stares, glaring with even more anger than before, at the woman walking away. Tap-tap-tap…

* * *

Ella heaves a sigh once she's alone, then she stares at the cleaning machine standing in the corner. She smirks. "I guess I can really surprise her by hurrying the work by using that monstrosity. But I do wish now Max was here to help me. I could have this floor done in under a day…"

Ella glances over her shoulder towards the stairs, hoping that any moment Max would arrive, but realises she's alone.

"Okay, I can do this. It was this knob to turn on this cleaning machine…"

Ella jumps back when cleaning machine comes to life with an almighty roar, and then once more when the sound echoes back at her from several directions.

"Hold on, stupid beast. If you are a 'Chase' machine, then you should be obeying *me*."

Sudden laughter behind Ella that she recognises. She turns and sees Max leaning against the wall.

"You plan on talking *that* into doing the cleaning for you?"

"How do you—"

"I overheard the conversation with the bitch."

"So, you help?"

"Only if you enlighten me by satisfying my curiosity."

"I'll try…"

18

***

"Do you want a burger and a cola? I can go get it. It's better than this crappy whatever this is that you're suggesting we're eating as lunch."

"That's what she leaves for me to have. Sometimes the workers are nice and leave me some of their food, but most of the time the bitch throws it into a bin before I can even get to it. I've never tasted cola. Is it nice?"

"Oh yes, but it's suggested not to drink too much of it…or so the doctors always say. I tend to ignore them." Max winks at Ella. "Want a burger and cola?"

Ella nods.

"I'll knock on the door downstairs when I'm back. Like this…"

Max knocks on the tread they're sitting on.

"Okay."

"I suggest you keep cleaning in case she arrives back. Or at least to give her the illusion you've been doing everything here all by yourself."

Ella gets up, and picks up the bucket beside her, "I wish I knew why she needs this place so clean. It can't be just because of the investors."

"Is that what she told you?"

"Yep."

"I'll be back as fast as possible."

***

Ella watches Max walk through car park outside towards the street beyond. It's a moment such as this when she wishes that she could do the same. She sighs, then turns and walks back to the bucket she'd placed on the floor for a moment, then walks to the banisters and using the small sponge starts scrubbing over it with the rough side, and by extension this action brings back Ella's earlier thoughts about why she needs to do the task and why she's even here.

Okay, get it together. Just remember you're not Cinderella. You're just an employee who's being mistreated by her employer. If I can even call the bitch an employer. Max said he's finding out what's going on. He asked about Dad too. I guess I just need to play along just like he said to do.

Two knocks.

"Is that you?"

"Yes, I suggest we eat outside the door, so the smell of this food doesn't spread around here. The *less* she can tie to you as bad behaviour the *better* it is for you."

"Okay, but I can't be outside for long." Ella rushes down the stairs and past Max, then flops down on the step. Max steps outside and grabs a bag and a bottle from the window frame beside the door.

"I decided to get a bottle, so it's easier to hide that you had *any* of this to drink. Just don't shake it, or it will explode out of the bottle. It's fizzy drink."

"Okay."

Max opens the bottle slowly then hands the bottle to Ella. She gingerly sips from the bottle, then looks surprised at Max, "It tastes funny. It feels like I got bubbles on my tongue. But I like it."

"Good. That solves one conundrum."

"What conundrum?"

"The conundrum of working out what sort of food and drink you'd *like*. Now this burger for example. It has a sauce on it. It *may* taste funny in a different way."

Ella takes hold of what she assumes is a burger, "Why

is the meat between the bread?"

"That's how it's served."

"Okay."

Looking sideways at Max just in case he plans to laugh at her, Ella opens her mouth open wide and then bites. This time the surprise is even greater and her head jerks sideways once more, and she stares with wide eyes at Max…

Chapter 5

MAX LAUGHS NONETHELESS WHEN HE sees the surprise on Ella's face. She grins too while chewing on the burger, then bursts out in a giggle for a few moments.

"Ah so you do know how to have fun…" Max reaches up and caresses the crease on Ella's face created by her broad smile. "I think that this suits you better than the angry frown I've seen so far, or the tears I saw yesterday."

"I don't have much to be happy about inside there." Ella whispers, nodding over her shoulder towards the door.

"I've noticed that."

"You said you wanted to satisfy your curiosity. I guess you want to ask me stuff."

"If you're okay with me asking. Remember earlier when I asked about your name?"

Ella nods.

"I asked because I saw something in her office, and I saw your name written on it."

"My name?"

"Yes, that's why I asked about your name. I think that something is going on here that may affect you."

"In what way?"

"I don't know. I'm only the cleaner. But I do want to help you because I can see you're sad about what has happened to you…and your father. I heard you mention him too."

"I miss him all the time. Even when my memories of him are so vague. He died for an unknown reason fifteen years ago."

"And your mother?"

"All I know is that she died when I was just a toddler. I was two or three at the time. My father married the *bitch* a year or so before he died."

"So, you don't even know your mother. That's sad."

"I miss her too even though I never knew her. I remember Dad telling me something about her being in the hospital for a year before she died there. I don't know how she died."

"I saw two women with the bitch when I arrived."

"Did they both have reddish brown hair like the bitch?"

"Yes, they did."

"That's my step-sisters. They bully me all the time and are as bad as their mother. I can't stand them. They're pretentious as hell. Don't let them fool you. They're as nasty as her and are as scheming as she is. I'm not stupid. I know that what they're doing must involve this place somehow. Especially when I saw that someone sanded off my name from the cleaning machine."

"That's why I suggested you use it. I wanted you to discover it."

"Thanks—I think."

"You're welcome. I find their treatment of you disgusting to say the least. I've been a cleaner here for three months, and when I saw you yesterday sitting in that chair, I think that was the first time I've ever seen you in the offices upstairs."

"Normally I don't dare to go there, but I do it each year on one specific day despite the risk. It would have been my dad's birthday yesterday."

"I see. You said it was your dad's chair, right? Does

she know that?"

"I hope not. Because if she did, she'd throw it out with everything else that was his. I have a few books that were his under my bed downstairs too. I just hope she'll never find them…"

"Give them to me. I'll keep them safe at my house."

"You have a house?"

"Of course. If you want, you could come with me, and I'll keep you hidden there if needed."

"Errr…that's nice, but—"

"But?"

"I need to stay here. If I go, they will end up unemployed. She knows she cannot get rid of them if I'm here. If I left, they would be in so much trouble."

Ella feels a familiar brushing over her cheek. She looks at Max who smiles at her gently. She sees compassion in his eyes. Without knowing why Ella feels her face become hot once again. *Shit, am I blushing?* She looks away, suddenly feeling extremely shy even though she'd talked frankly with Max about rather personal matters.

"Max, can I ask you something?"

"Go ahead."

"What would you do if it was you in this situation?"

"To be honest, I don't know because I've never experienced something like this. I think you're brave. Just remember that I'm working on fixing this, okay. I can't yet tell you how, but I know things will be okay for you in a few days."

"I hope so."

"I know so, Ella. Just hold on. Remember that you're not alone anymore. You got me."

Max leans sideways and kisses Ella on her forehead, causing Ella to blush once more. And more. This time she feels a tingly feeling coursing through her body like she has never felt before.

Is this how falling in love might feel? Am I falling in love with him? Is he my Prince Max who will rescue me from my evil step-

***

Ella finishes off her burger, then she drinks a few more sips from the cola. She hands the bottle to Max who tightens the cap, then puts the bottle in his bag. "I'll take it home with me and use the bin in the street for these wrappings." Max nods towards the gate beyond which cars are now driving past. "It's close to rush hour, so it means that she'll think I've just arrived to work. If we work fast, we can be done with it before she's here."

"Okay, but she'll still want me repairing the junk too."

"As yesterday I'll help with it. I said you're *not* alone anymore. I'll help with everything now until it's time—"

Max walks off before Ella can ask a meaning for the words. She stares after him, again wondering why at times he sounds so mysterious. She just hopes that he's not someone working for the bitch because that would mean she'd be in serious trouble now.

A few minutes pass before Max is back, but his bag is gone now. Ella gets up, and steps back into the factory, followed by Max who closes the door softly.

Chapter 6

ELLA WALKS SLOWLY ALONG THE upper floor of the offices, and glances through the window of each office cubicle at the content of each 'room' before she sprays the window thoroughly with cleaning liquid. She tries to imagine herself sitting in one of the rooms as an employee, but she can't bring herself to imagine a normal life.

Not yet at least. Not until it's two days from now. I hope Max spoke the truth when he said he was getting things sorted.

When she investigates the next cubicle, Ella grins. She sees a book on the desk. A book that has a story in it that is all too like her own situation. After looking in each direction, Ella opens the door of the cubicle and rushes inside, closing the door behind her. She listens for sounds. When she hears none, she lunges for the book.

Ella caresses the cover of the book that's made of soft leather. On its cover a single word is imprinted into the leather with gold leaf: *Cinderella*.

"I wonder whose office this is?" Ella murmurs. "This is beautiful."

Ella sits down on a chair behind the desk, and she places the book on her legs. Again, she caresses over the cover, then opens it. On the first page she sees a beautiful print depicting a woman in a long, pale-blue dress with one of her legs stretched out and a man kneeling before her, putting a shoe onto her foot.

"This is so beautiful. I wonder whose book is this is. I guess it won't harm anyone if I read this book later when I know the bitch has gone home."

"Ella."

Ella glances up when she hears Max call her name, "I'm over here." Ella calls out. She hears some fast-paced footsteps, then Max appears in the doorway.

"What are you doing in here? Never mind. I just saw the *bitch* pull up, so you need to hurry down to the repair room. I can keep *her* busy until you're not out of breath anymore."

Ella places the book quickly back on the desk and sprints past Max towards the workload elevator that would take her to the cellar where the repair room is located. Before leaving, Max looks at the book on the desk. He frowns when he sees the name of it. He walks to the desk and places the book upside down on the desk. *Best not have the bitch see this book or she might get ideas from it. I wonder if Ella was reading it because she's starting to realise about her situation.*

* * *

Max walks quickly walks to the elevator that would be used by Mrs Chase and calls the elevator up. With the elevator on the top floor, *she* would need to wait for it to arrive down again, and the elevator is slow as it is. Two minutes later the elevator arrives, and Max grabs the vacuum cleaner and makes a point of vacuuming the floor of the elevator, and the heavy vacuum cleaner prevents the door from closing for a time. Once that's done, he lifts the vacuum cleaner into the elevator, unplugs it from the socket and walks into the elevator before the doors close.

It takes just two more minutes to arrive downstairs, and a surprised Mrs Chase stares at him while he stares back cold at her.

"What are you doing in my elevator?" Mrs Chase snaps at him. "Who are you?"

"I'm the night cleaner." Max states pointedly.

"Who hired you?"

"Your employment department did."

"Oh—Anyway, go clean somewhere else. The noise of vacuums gives me a headache."

"I'm required to clean the lobby according to my schedule."

"Then get on with it. Spick and span."

"You have an interesting way with words. I guess you're the darling of everyone who works for you."

"I'm not interested in being a darling of anyone."

Mrs Chase walks into the elevator, turns and frowns when she sees Max grinning at her. She grunts, then pushes the button to allow her to go up. Max looks up at the sign above the elevator doors and sees the number counting.

"That gives Ella fifteen or twenty minutes. Enough time for me to go help her after cleaning. I best give the impression I'm doing what she thinks."

Max turns, switches on the vacuum and makes a point of vacuuming in front of the elevator just in case Mrs Chase wants to come pester him.

After a few minutes, Max turns the vacuum off, pushes the button to bring the elevator down, then he walks nonchalantly away towards the stairs leading downstairs, then after arriving he rushes down until he's in the cellar. A few minutes later he walks into the repair room, and grins at Ella who smiles when she sees him.

"I think I'm getting better at this thanks to your

lessons." Ella beams a broader smile at Max.

"Good. I can help a few minutes. The bitch went up to her office, but I doubt she'll stay there for long."

"I'll try to work faster. For once I want to be finished before she arrives."

"You will with my help."

Silently both work on the equipment needing to be repaired, but then Max looks up from his own work when he hears Ella grunt, "What's wrong, Ella?"

"I just saw something that makes me angry as hell all the sudden. On this equipment. Like the cleaning machine someone removed the name…"

"Let me see."

Ella hands the wire bundle to Max. "It's on the left side, next to the black wires."

"Ah right, I see what you mean. I got an idea. I have my cell phone with me today. I can take a photo of this."

"What use is that?"

"It can act as proof of what she's doing to you."

"I guess so. But I doubt the cops will even believe me if I go to them. I'm never going to get out of this place…"

Chapter 7

Ella slumps on the repair desk, burying her head into her folded arms that are already wet from a flood of tears that came as soon as she said the words. She feels a hand on her back. Max gently lifts her face until she's facing him. He looks at her with a stern expression.

"I told you not to give up. It's *less* than two days, and then something is going to happen. Can you hold on that long?"

"I can try."

Max looks up with a frown on his face, "I think I can hear her walking through the corridor upstairs. I'll sit down over there in the corner. I have an idea."

"Okay."

"Don't worry. If she tries to do something I can help you, okay."

Ella nods.

Max walks towards the chair in the corner of the room behind Ella who glances at him for a moment, then looks towards the door...

Tap-tap-tap.

Ella feels a wave of fear go over her when the door opens, and her step-mother enters the room. They stare at one another, and strangely, for once, it is her step-mother who looks away. She stares incredulously at the table.

"You're already finished—" she mutters.

"I guess this batch was easy. Except for—" Ella begins to say. She's uncertain what to say next. A loud snoring sound interrupts her, and it seems both she and her step-mother have the same need to look behind where Ella is sitting. On the sofa behind her, Max seemingly sleeps.

"I thought—"

Ella glances back at her step-mother, noting an uncommon hesitation in her voice.

"Anyway, if you're done *here*, I have another task for you. Perhaps the idiot behind you can help *too*."

Ella snaps back to reality when her step-mother speaks in an icy cold tone suddenly. She promptly turns and this time the taps of her heels are faster than usual.

* * *

"Okay, that was normal and strange at the same time." Ella says, after silently staring at the doorway for five minutes. "I wonder what's different."

"She couldn't speak to you in her normal way because I'm here." Max quietly voices. "She knows that I'm a witness now. Plus, also this…"

Max holds up his cell phone, "I recorded the conversation. I have both a video and her talking. I'm going to venture a guess that the 'task' she spoke of is to throw out evidence of what she did against your father and against you."

"How do you know that?"

"I've watched enough cop shows to know."

"Oh right."

Ella glances back at the repair desk and all the fixed devices there. She picks up the device where she'd spotted the removal of the company name 'Chase'. She holds it up and turns to Max, "Do you think this means she's doing a crime here? This and the cleaning machine—"

"Yes."

Max rises from the seating and walks to the repair desk. He accepts the device from Ella and looks it over once she points at the location of the missing company name, "Yes, it's clear that someone scraped off four letters."

"It's supposed to be my father's business. Well, actually mine."

"Yes, it should *all* be yours. I'm guessing that *her* 'task' involves destroying the proof of that. We best go upstairs and see what she wants you to *do*, with me helping you. I'll try to make sure she cannot go ahead with anything she has planned."

Ella gets up and once she stands, Max takes her by the shoulders. He looks at her face searchingly before he speaks again, "I saw the book you were looking at. This isn't a fairy tale you're in. It's a dangerous situation. She *is* dangerous. It seems she made you disappear for fifteen years."

"No one knows about me outside this place?" Ella whispers.

"Before yesterday—no. But now they *do*. I told them."

"I wasn't expecting it to be like a fairy tale with me being rescued by a handsome prince."

Max smirks, "So I'm not handsome enough for you then?"

"I didn't say that."

"I know. But—"

Max stops speaking and leans forward and kisses Ella on her lips before he speaks once more, "But I guess you may not like me anyway once you know my true identity."

Ella frowns but decides not to ask why Max would make such a comment.

Before either can break the awkward silence that suddenly descends on them, they hear a voice echo through the corridor that neither wants to hear, "Ellaaaa. Spick and span—"

* * *

Both Ella and Max feel like children being chastised as they walk into her step-mother's office. They're met with a cold, hard stare. Ella feels Max's hand touch hers. It allows Ella to relax somewhat.

"If the two of you want to play pranks, there are consequences for that sort of behaviour. As I said this morning, I need to make this place perfect for the investors. The offices are too much of a mess to my liking. I want *both* of you to collect all unnecessary paperwork, books, junk…and throw it all down the chute so it all goes into the dumpster downstairs."

"Yes, Mrs Chase." Max answers.

"Yes, mother." Ella whispers.

"I'm going now. I have dinner planned with my two daughters."

Both Max and Ella stay silent until the fast-paced tap-tap-tap has faded from earshot, then Max whispers the precise thought going through Ella's mind, "She doesn't even regard you as a daughter."

"I guess she never has." Ella whispers back. "I guess it proves even more how right you are about all *this*. Whatever all *this* is really."

"I have some friends—That dumpster isn't going to rid her of evidence, if you get what I mean. Let me call someone quick. It's best you stand out there in case she comes back."

Ella frowns a moment then she nods. Once outside the office, she listens to the murmur coming from within. The call doesn't last long…

Chapter 8

MAX NODS AT ELLA WHEN he walks from the office. Despite having another moment of doubt about him, Ella feels relief wash over her, *I guess I'll have to trust him. But I wonder what's with all the questions he keeps asking me. No cleaner needs to know this much…*

"Where do you want to start?"

Ella glances around. Her gaze fixes first on the door of her step-mother's office, then the two for her step-sisters, and then finally on the door where she'd found the book earlier.

"I think, and I'm not an expert, that if you swapped dumpsters so evidence goes somewhere safe, that the first evidence would be the paperwork in the offices of the bitch and her two daughters. Yes, you're right I'm *not* her daughter. I'm my dad's daughter. Then there's certain things I want safe from her antics as well."

"Okay, it's your call. I'm just here to help. I guess I deserve this after the way I spoke to *her* earlier."

"What did you say?"

"Not so much what I said, but how I surprised her by using her precious elevator. Have you never seen how stupidly silly she's about touching stuff? Last time she touched something dirty it was almost like she could have placed her hand on a hot stove."

"I had noticed it. I thought it was because of me."

"There are people out there, who feel fearful of touching dirty stuff. I think she's one of them. A few of such people, can also become unreasonable at times with others, while wanting to keep stuff clean. Not going to say this is what she has but the symptoms are there."

"If she's sent to prison, I hope they give her the dirtiest cell in there."

"When—"

Ella looks at Max, then softly repeats the word, "When—"

* * *

A whistle pierces through the air, and Ella jerks up and she looks towards the open window, "What was that?"

"Our signal. Once we've collected all the evidence, and the things *you* want to save from *her* wrath, they'll take the current dumpster with those items away and replace it with one containing another company's junk, and then we complete the task here. She'll be none the wiser, and unless the bitch digs down to the bottom of the dumpster or gets her precious daughters to climb in to do it for her, she'll never know what we did here."

"Those precious daughters better take off their expensive shoes covered with Swarovski gems, or they'd be totally ruined in the experience. The last time they tried to do anything remotely close to cleaning, one of them, can't recall who now, lost a shoe down the chute and she was in a right panic until one of the employees had found it. The shoe was ruined. Then as she stepped into the shoe, she cut off her toe almost because of a piece of glass that had gone inside the shoe during it descend."

Max laughs.

"If I didn't know better, the more I hear about your oh-so-dysfunctional step-family the more I feel like I'm caught up in a modern-day version of the Cinderella story. No pun intended, and no insult meant by it."

"None taken. I think the same. Especially now with you here. No pun or insult intended either."

"One difference though. I think it's more likely that *you* will be doing the rescuing in the end, not me."

They're silent as they walk into the next office to clean up: the one belonging to the oldest of the two step-sisters. Max grabs a pile of paperwork from the highest shelf and hands it to Ella who places it on the desk.

"Did she need stitches for the toe?"

"Errr—Haven't you noticed how *odd* her shoes look. Some of the employees claim half her toe is missing."

"It may sound harsh, but in a way, it will teach her. Vanity *never* gets its just reward. Neither does cruelty and—"

"I wonder why she has a photo of my dad and I here?"

Max turns and see Ella holding up a photo. He walks over and looks down at the faded photo that shows a toddler on her father's shoulder, "That's you I guess."

"Yes, I remember this photo from childhood. I wondered where it went after—"

Max places a hand on Ella's shoulder, "We'll figure it all out once this is over, okay."

Ella nods, then feels a hand caress her cheek. She looks up and sees something new in Max's eyes. Something that betrays his feelings for her.

I guess falling in love isn't simply two people saying 'I love you' to one another. It's about two people sharing something profound and growing closer like we are. Am I falling in love with him too? My face doesn't feel hot anymore when he looks at me like this...

* * *

It's just after midday when the last of the evidence disappears down the chute. Ella suddenly feels like a weight is lifted from her shoulders, *If I can make it through the rest of today and then tomorrow, everything will be over. He says so.*

"Right, shall we see if the floor below has anything important too?"

"My Dad's old office is there. She keeps it locked though."

"I'm the cleaner here. I have a master key for all doors."

"Yes, let's go there next. But what about his chair? It won't fit down the chute."

"I'll carry it down and tell one of them downstairs to place it in the truck they have with them. It will be just as safe."

"Please do. It's the only thing I have left that's special. He told me my mother purchased it when he got the patent granted. Yes, I know about that because I've been reading through the paperwork we collected in the bitch's office."

Ella is about to walk towards the stairs when Max stops her, "No, Ella. This place, all of it, is yours. We go down in that..."

Max nods towards the elevator. Ella swallows hard, looks at Max who nods at her encouragingly, then she nods and slowly walks towards the elevator.

Chapter 9

ELLA STANDS CLOSE TO MAX as they both stare up at the display telling them that the elevator is on its way. There's nothing to stop them from having to confront Mrs Chase if she's standing inside the elevator once the doors slide open. The tension makes Ella's heartbeat faster inside her chest. She feels her body tremble. She knows it's forbidden for her to go on this elevator…

She feels Max's hand grip tighter around her own. She feels a renewed surge of courage, *I can do this. All this is mine.* The thought repeats itself in sync with the counting of the elevator's display. She heaves a deep sigh when the elevator is empty once the doors open a minute later.

"Come."

Ella doesn't hesitate. She knows that now there's no turning back. *Whatever we're doing, it's now in motion, and I must remember that tomorrow is my last day here like this. Tomorrow she'll pay for what she did to my dad and to me.*

The doors close and Ella can't help herself and she smiles when a soft tune starts, "That was my dad's favourite piece of classical music." Ella whispers. "I wonder now how the bitch feels every time she's in this elevator."

"It definitely taunts *her*. She didn't look happy when

she stepped into this elevator earlier. I guess it's your father's way of being able to keep taunting *her* despite his passing, so I'm guessing that he discovered that she wasn't the right woman for him. Maybe their marriage was him being on the rebound because he was still grieving your mother's passing. It makes it even clearer to *me* that something happened and that she's involved in it directly."

"Maybe Dad wanted to divorce *her*, but she did something that caused him to die."

Ella gasps and presses her hands over her mouth. She stares with wide-open eyes at Max, "Did I just say that?" Ella mumbles from behind her hands.

"You did. And unfortunately, you may be right."

* * *

Another period silence accompanies their walk towards the room where Ella had been sitting just a few days earlier when she'd encountered Max in person for the first time. As they arrive at the room Max and Ella look at each other before walking inside.

Ella sits down in the chair and runs her hand along the side of the chair, "I miss him so much."

"I understand you miss him, but you need to look forward not back."

"I know. I guess I'll have to come to terms with whatever happened to him."

Max squats down and holds his hand against Ella's cheek, "You're not alone anymore. I'll help you through *this* until it's over. I cannot tell you more than that, and I *do* hope that you're not going to think less of me when the truth *does* come out. Remember this regardless of what happens. Truth always prevails when people try to lie or cheat their way into situations such as what your step-mother and step-sisters are doing. It will all work out, okay.”

“Okay…”

“Anyway, let me carry this chair downstairs. You stay here, and please wait until I’m back. Hide somewhere if the *bitch* turns up, and if that happens just stay silent.”

Ella nods.

Max straightens up, and Ella gets up, though somewhat reluctantly. She nods, then watches Max pick up the chair without any effort. Suddenly she realises how strong Max really is, so when he said he could protect her he means it. She watches Max walk from the room, then looks around in a panic for a moment before rushing to the window to look outside.

After several minutes have passed, Ella sees Max far below her, carrying the chair to a vehicle where two men seem to greet him like they know him. *I wonder who they are. They seem to know him.* Ella smiles when she sees the chair being handled like it’s the most precious object ever, like an expensive painting was being carried and not her father’s old chair.

“I guess I’m liking him more and more. He kissed me. I wonder how he really feels about me…”

Ella turns and walks to the table and walks past the piles of paper lying on the desk, all of which are covered in dust. It’s obvious that this room hasn’t been used for years. Ella looks at the end of the long table, and for a moment she can imagine her father sitting there.

“I better make sure that I collect all this paperwork as well while I’m here. It may prove this company is mine.”

Ella picks up the first pile of paper and blows the dust from it. She sees a date on the top of the first sheet of paper. “That date is more than fifteen years ago. What happened here for this to be left behind, and then for Dad to die so suddenly.”

Ella looks up when she hears footsteps, but as they lacked the distinct taps of the heels of the sort of shoes her step-mother or step-sisters wear, she feels some relief. A moment after, Max enters the room.

"I found something here."

Max walks around the table to where Ella stands, still holding the pile of dusty stack of paper in her hands. She hands them to Max, who looks over the page.

"A date."

"I saw it too."

"It could give some evidence in finding out what your step-mother did fifteen years ago. We can add this to the items we're extracting from this place."

"Are those two men going to take it all somewhere safe? I saw you talking to them."

"Yes, they are also helping. I best wait with saying how until after tomorrow, okay."

Ella nods, then stares around the room in a pensive mood, before she continues, "I usually have trouble trusting people because of how the bitch treats me, but with you…"

"You trust me?"

"I actually do."

"Hopefully, that won't change…"

Chapter 10

ELLA YAWNS AND FOR A change, she had the chance to sleep through the night because of Max's suggestion for him to be 'on duty' as he'd stated. She stretches, then stares at the window, and sees sunlight streaming in.

"What time is it?" she mutters.

"Time for breakfast." Ella smiles when Max's voice echoes from the repair room. A moment later Ella becomes aware of something smelling sweet.

"What breakfast?" she calls out.

"I got it over here on the repair desk. I wonder if I should eat it *all*. There's no way you'll enjoy pancakes for breakfast."

"Pancakes? You got pancakes?"

"Yes, I have pancakes. Let's see—one, two, three, four, five, six for me if you don't hurry up and get here."

Ella jolts up from the bed, puts on her clothes, then she rushes next door where she abruptly stops. She stares in amazement at the repair desk which is devoid of any equipment to be repaired or any tools lying there usually. Over it lies a linen tablecloth on which sits a large plate with a stack of pancakes on top of it. Next to it sits a small bowl with fruit, a bottle of what she guesses is a bottle containing syrup of some sort, and small plate of butter.

"My Dad used to do pancakes when I was little." Ella blurts out. She feels a sudden hunger pang. The next moment, Ella feels her face hot from blushing, when her stomach makes an audible gurgling sound. It's met with a wave of laughter from Max.

"Come. Sit. My mother made these pancakes when she heard about you from me last night. Your father's chair is now a guest in her spare room, and she said to me that you're welcome to come live with her until you get everything sorted out to start afresh, once this is over."

"Really? That's really nice of her."

"You'll meet her tomorrow afternoon. And the offer stands regardless of how you may view *me* after tomorrow."

Ella decides not to ask for the meaning of the words. Instead, she smiles warmly at Max, then sits down at the repair desk and looks at the food. She feels hesitant about taking any of it.

"If the *bitch* comes, I'll make sure she leaves you alone."

"Okay."

"Now, how many pancakes do you want? I got more in that container over there." Max nods sideways towards the wall. Ella sees a box on the floor.

"I think I start with two."

"I'll take two as well."

Ella looks at the remaining food on the repair desk.

"This bottle has maple syrup in it. It's from Canada. My mother has her sister send it over from there from time to time."

"Your mother is from Canada?"

"She is."

"How did you end up here?"

"I guess my mother decided to let my father decide where the money was best."

"Is that why he wanted you to be an electrical engineer?"

"I guess so, but that's a rather long story. *Too* long for a romantic breakfast with the bravest woman I know."

"I'm not brave."

"I think you are. Anyway, let's continue. This fruit here is a mixture of berries from my mother's garden. The way I like to have my pancakes is as follows…"

Ella watches on as Max places a spoonful of the fruit on each of his pancakes, then pours some of the syrup over it, then places a thin slice of the butter on top. He rolls each pancake tight. She copies all his actions.

"Try it." Max says, beaming a smile at her.

Ella complies, and her face displays a broad smile a moment later, "That's delicious."

* * *

Ella is about to place the first bite of her fifth pancake into her mouth when she hears a sound that makes her cringe to the core.

Tap-tap-tap.

Not just one person's footsteps, but *three*. A moment later, she stares at her step-mother and step-sisters, who all stare back, first surprised, then annoyed, then all three displaying a mirror image contortion of anger.

Max and Ella stare at the newcomers, then at one another, before both burst out laughing loud uncontrollably.

"What *is* going on here? Ella, who gave permission for *you* to be slacking. What is *this* food doing here?"

"It's our breakfast. I think *we* have a plan to have a day of *fun* today."

"Mother why are you letting *her* talk that way?"

"Yes, how dare you speak to *me* in this manner. I'm

your mother and—"

"No, you're not. You are a step-bitch."

"Mother."

Ella giggles then looks at her step-sisters, "Not so much fun when you're *not* in control, huh? I guess I can decide later what the employees will be doing when they arrive."

"It's *our* company."

"No, Mrs Chase, this is actually *her* company, and before that it was her father's company. None of you three has *any* claim to it. Not if I go by some of the paperwork I've seen."

"Shut up, you're just a cleaner here."

"I guess I can clean up this place some more. It seems I missed some dirt right here. Want me to clean this place up some more, Ellana?"

"Her name is *Ella*."

"It's Ellana Chase, and you know it, you *bitch*. And this place belonged to *my* father, and now it's mine."

"And now *who* is going to believe you, Ellaaaa…"

Ella stares at the younger of her step-sisters with equal venom that she's seeing in the woman's face. Maybe in another life, and other circumstances they might have been friends, but not now and certainly after what the other woman's mother had possibly done fifteen years ago…

Ella is about to speak again when she feels Max's hand grasp hers and squeeze it softly. She quickly looks at him and sees him shake ever so gently. She turns her face back to the three women opposite her, but she stares blankly at the fire hose beyond them to focus on something other than them. She shuts her mind, also, to the taunts coming now from all three…

Chapter 11

WHEN THE SOUND OF THREE pairs of high-heeled shoes finally fade in the distance, Ella finally relaxes and slumps forward. She bursts into a flood of tears, "I told you. There's *no* way I can *ever* get away from them. They hate me and what they said *will* happen. Once you're gone they *will* make sure I'll regret eating these pancakes, and what I said to them all…"

Ella looks silently at Max, now with the earlier doubts back in her mind about him, and curious also how he plans to explain what he'd hinted at. Max seems to stare at his plate, seemingly shy now. Ella places her hand gently over his hand. He looks up at Ella.

"I guess I said stuff you're wondering about."

"I'm wondering about it, but I guess I can *wait* until tomorrow for answers. I guess I need to *trust* you."

"Okay, sweetheart."

Ella looks surprised when Max answers in a tone like how he'd spoken to her on the first evening. She backs away.

"Max…"

"Yes?"

"What's going on?"

"I guess I'm preparing myself rejection…"

Max gets up, and stomps from the room. Ella stares after him in astonishment, then looks at the table. She reaches over the repair desk to something she recognises as belonging to Max. He'd forgotten his wallet…

Ella feels tempted to open the wallet. Opening it would offer the immediate answer of *who* Max really is, and perhaps *why* he's here. She starts to unfold the square object, but Ella only makes it a quarter inch into the action before she snaps the wallet shut and gently, like she's handling a fragile object, places it back in the place it had been lying. She pulls her arm away, and stares at the door and listens for any footsteps that indicates Max coming back.

No sounds.

Silence permeates Ella's surroundings. Like the building had become abandoned. She listens for sounds from outside. She can't hear any cars driving by, and glancing at the clock on the wall and seeing it's only a minute before the 9 AM bus would drive by, stop for a few seconds then move on… The ticking of the clock goes past the moment that this arrival of the bus would happen. Silence everywhere…

Ella sighs, then glances around at the small repair room, and then at the door of the room that was her designated 'bedroom', though the circumstance of the massive workload given by Mrs Chase often meant she didn't, or more precisely, couldn't use it.

She gets up and walks to the door. After a final longing stare at the repair table that had been so romantic until the arrival of Mrs Chase and her two daughters. Suddenly, the breakfast felt off, almost like dressing up for pretence.

Ella gags, and a moment later she throws up. The impact of the situation causes a renewed fear to well up. Something about it seems like she was being fooled into believing things would change, "Maybe Max isn't even his real name. Maybe *he* was sent here to test *me*. To make sure I would be obedient. No Prince Max for *you*."

No prince of any kind for you, Ellana Chase.

Ella walks to the bed in the corner of the room. She slumps down and pushes herself into a tight ball. A thought repeats itself in her mind despite every effort to ward it off, "But I love him, but I love him, but I love him…"

The emotion of what happened during the morning causes Ella to become exhausted and an hour later she falls asleep without noticing it…

* * *

Ella wakes a few hours later, and stares at the window. The dusk betrays an immediate difference between this day and any previous days.

"It was supposed to happen today…" Ella whispers. "Where's Max? Why can't I hear any of the machines working?"

Ella pushes herself up using the wall for balance. She feels a dizzying nausea overcome her for a moment, and realises that she'd last eaten early that morning, and then had thrown it all up. Leaning against the wall, she moves towards the door, uncertain what she might find outside it. She steps into something wet with her bare foot, and realises her puke is still on the floor. She glances at the repair table…

"It's all still there. Even the wallet."

Ella jerks when her own voice sounds loud. She listens for any reactions from outside in case someone was waiting for her to awaken. Still that same silence…

She walks to the table where three, now cold, pancakes lie on the large plate. She grabs one and mechanically chews from it while staring intently at the wallet. That wallet, which could offer her all the immediate answers. *Why am I so afraid to look inside it? I guess it's a bit like Cinderella's shoe. It belongs to the 'chosen one', except, it seems, I'm becoming like the prince. Does it mean that I could prove to Max, I truly love him if I don't look inside it? If I don't do that, then let the truth come out, and then give him it and do it without ever looking inside…*

Ella puts half the pancake not yet eaten down on the plate. She reaches for the wallet once more and holds it against her chest. She lets her fingers caress the surface, then brings it to her nose and smells real leather.

"I guess he cares about the chair for *other* reasons than just to be nice. This shows he cares about how he comes over to everyone around him. I guess he won me over with his behaviour and caring for me, not by saying a hollow 'I love you' to me."

Ella jerks and drops the wallet on the chair beside her when she hears footsteps approach. A few moments later, she stares at the foreman of the factory, who seems tired, withdrawn, and awkward in his mannerisms. For a moment, Ella expects the usual short, barked comment that he'd always convey to her on behalf of Mrs Chase telling her that day's tasks.

"I was sent down. They want you up in an hour…"

The foreman is gone before Ella can respond his words. The words leave her frozen in place and wondering again what's going on.

Chapter 12

Ella glances around the corner of the doorway to the repair room into the corridor and finds it empty. She's met with the silence that she'd noticed after waking. She looks behind her at the wallet on the chair, then dashes to it and places it into the pocket of her long shirt.

Slowly, Ella walks towards the elevator, almost afraid that it will open, and her step-mother will emerge from it to taunt her even more.

"No, I can't let them bully me anymore. I *must* do something to stop all this, but what? And how? Will Max really help as he said? I wonder why he's afraid of my reaction of what goes on up there…"

Ella stops a few feet away from the elevator. She stares at the doors, "If I go to the top floor that's where Max kissed me for the first time. Not a kiss of lusting for something more, but that gentle caring kiss by someone who cares about a person's feelings. A gentle kiss by someone who's been caring about me a long time. He says he's been here three months. He must have seen me here. But he's letting me decide whether I want to be with him. If that's true, that's like true love I would guess."

Ella walks forward and pushes her finger against the button. She glances up at the display, and almost in slow motion the numbers count down. Too slow in her mind. She wants to be upstairs now. To find out for real if her mind is telling her the truth about Max's feelings, or that it had tricked her in a lull of false hope.

A soft pinging sound announces the lift. She steps inside, stiffens up and at first can't bring herself to push the second uppermost button. Slowly her hand reaches out. She closes her eyes then pushes…

Another pinging sound causes Ella to open her eyes. She sees the familiar glass panels that divide the upper floor into the illusion of separate offices. She looks around for the presence of people, but all the cubicles are devoid of the usual staff. From what seems a far-off distance, she hears a murmur of voices drifting towards her.

Ella becomes aware of someone walking towards her from the left. A petite woman with black hair stops next to her and seems hesitant speaking to her, "Please…come. I was…told to bring you to a place to wait."

Ella nods curtly. She follows the woman, who seems unwilling to engage in a conversation. The woman points at a doorway, and Ella guesses that's the room she needs to use for waiting.

But for how long? And what? And for whom? Why…?

At first, Ella decides to stare at the windows, and for a moment contemplates looking through them to see if she could see the vehicle outside the building which Max had approached with the chair. And if it was there whether the two men were there too. And if they were there that perhaps Max might be standing there talking to them…

But Ella stays sitting. Something stops her from moving. Perhaps it's the fear of finding out what's going on, or perhaps because in that moment she was hearing something familiar that causes a chill to rise over her body, and her hair stand up and her skin to cover itself in goose bumps.

"Ella is the one behind this scheme to make me into the villain, isn't she? She did all this. If she thinks she gets any of this, she's more deluded that any of you. Maybe I should get her arrested for…for…for…something…goddammit…"

"What the hell is the bitch trying to claim about me?" Ella hisses between her teeth. She perks up, and now listens intently to what's happening. Now her attention is entirely focused on the sounds coming from the other side of the offices, from the direction of her father's old office. From the place, where the day earlier, his old leather chair had been located. Where dusty paperwork had shown Ella that the *true* ownership of Chase Industries should be hers, and *not* be in the hands of her evil step-mother or her evil step-sisters, whose whiny voices now also become louder, and filled with protest like that of Mrs Chase.

Ella hears a booming voice call out, "I suggest you stop speaking, Angela. You're the one who brought this on your own head with all your scheming that you started the day you married Roger."

"Roger." Ella blurts out loud. "That's Dad's name."

Ella jerks her head around, and looks at the doorway, fearful that anyone might have heard her. No one comes.

So, this is about me, but I had it all the wrong way around. That man, and the others I can hear, are doing something to stop her. I didn't even know her name is Angela.

Ella glances around, then rushes to a chair near the window. She doesn't want anyone to realise she'd heard the words. But as she flops down in the chair, she also realises something profound, *Max spoke the truth. He did help me. So, when he said he loves me and doesn't know how I'll feel about him today, he was worried I'd reject him for helping them. I need to go to him. If he's here at all. If he's here I'll give him the wallet. I'll tell him I love him too. And then——*

Ella isn't sure what would be next…

* * *

Ella takes a sip from the cup of hot soup given to her by another of the office workers, though in her hazy mind Ella is having trouble remembering the woman's name. She notices a grimace on the woman's face before she walks away. It makes Ella aware that something is going on that may not be so benevolent in nature. Ella reaches up to her face, expecting tears to be flowing down her cheeks

I guess I miss Max. Hang on, what am I thinking. I miss Max, because—Why do I miss him so much? He's hiding something about himself that worries him, but I guess I've started to love him because of how he treats me, speaks to me, and helps me…

"Ella."

Chapter 13

ELLA LOOKS UP AND SEES the foreman from the factory stand in the doorway. She sees a scowl on his face, but she realises that it's caused by irrational worry on his part, "Do you know what's going on in there?"

"Sorry, no."

"The others say that they're going to close this place, and that she's moving overseas with them."

"You mean the bitch?"

"Yes, *her*. She's in there talking with the investors, but she doesn't look happy. She was screaming at them, and I heard her use *your* name…"

"My—name?"

"Yes, she said to them that the disappeared money was *your* fault. Do you know what she's on about?"

"Errr—no. Sorry. I can't help you."

"Fair enough. Just *be* careful…I was told you need to bring Max here."

The foreman walks off, leaving Ella alone with renewed worries in her mind, which increases as she listens to the sounds from the other room. Above the sounds of all those talking, the sound of her step-mother's screams is the loudest.

"She sounds like she's being tortured or something."

Ella murmurs. "Well, I guess that after the way she's treated me, she deserves to be locked up in a tiny cell the same size as the one I had to use, with the same sort of food she always gave me, and I guess she can stay there for the rest of her life…"

Ella jolts up from the chair and for a moment she's uncertain what to do, but then she stares at the doorway. Slowly she walks towards it. When she reaches it, she stares down the hallway towards where the rowdy discussion is coming. The hallway is empty.

"I guess I can go rescue Max. Never mind, whatever his secret *is*. I love him. I'm certain he feels the same about *me*…"

* * *

"A**re *you* going to keep polishing that window, or shall I rescue *you* from this job, Max?" Ella grins when Max turns around. "I could carry out of here like in that movie, errr, what was it called again?"

"You mean like in the movie 'An Officer and A Gentleman'?" Max laughs loud. "Are you up for carrying me like that?"

"I guess I can't carry you, but you *can* come *with* me. If those lawyers up there are right, you're on *my* payroll so…you can come with me upstairs. I want someone I *trust* there with me, while they listen to the sore excuses the bitch and her kiddos are telling the lawyers about what the hell, they've been doing for the last fifteen years."

"You want to find out what they did to your father?"

"Yes, actually.!"

"Even if it points at something bad?"

Ella frowns for a moment, "Do you think something bad happened?"

"Only way to find out is to go upstairs. I'll go with

you, but you need to be prepared for surprises, okay."

"Okay."

Max walks close to Ella and stops in front of her. He lifts her face with a finger and looking searchingly into her eyes, "You got your father's eye colour."

"How do you—" Ella can't finish the sentence because Max presses his lips against hers. Ella's eyes fly open wide, and for a moment she squirms. But it doesn't take long for her mind to shift to the events of a few nights earlier when Max had kissed her forehead. She feels her face become hot and is certain that she's blushing. A few minutes pass, then Max slowly moves away from her.

"I guess that first time when I kissed you a few nights ago, it wasn't good enough to show how I feel. I've been here for weeks, and I managed to fall head over heels in love with you in that time. But I'll let you decide if you feel the same about me *after* we've gone upstairs, okay."

Ella nods, and for a moment feels a pang of fear rise about whatever it is she's about to discover about Max.

"I have something of yours…" Ella says hesitantly.

"Something of mine?" Max stares surprised at Ella.

"Yes, this." Ella smiles when she sees Max's face go from surprise to fear, "It's not a glass shoe obviously"

Max grins at Ella, then looks again at his wallet, and frowns.

"I didn't open it."

"Errr…okay."

Ella smiles when she sees Max blush as bright as perhaps, she'd done herself before, when he had caught her off guard, "Should I look? Okay, so what secrets does 'Prince Max' keep in his precious wallet. Perhaps a discount card for a shoe shop for a secret shoe fetish…"

Max looks again at Ella and sees her grinning broadly.

"I'm trying to tell you it's okay to surprise me. By now nothing surprises me anymore. Unless it's a revelation that you're the bitch's brother's nephew's cousin's former roommate, then I think you're perfectly okay…"

"You've seen that movie?"

"Yes, secretly. I think one of them who works in the offices upstairs took pity on me for having boring nights with nothing to do. She left her cell phone behind on purpose. On the screen it said, 'Click the button, watch the movie, have a night of giggles.'

"I love that movie…"

"I guess we got something in common it seems."

∗ ∗ ∗

Max takes hold of Ella's hand and pulls her closer. He reaches up to her face and caresses her cheek with the back of his hand. He leans forward and kisses gently on Ella's forehead. He looks down at Ella, and she sees some concern flash over his face for a moment, before he speaks again, "Let's go."

"Okay, I guess I'll have to face the music at some point."

"It's not going to be bad. I promise…"

"Then why are you worried?"

"I guess—I think I'll have to explain when we get upstairs. It's no accident you were told to come downstairs for me. It was planned that this would happen in this way, so they can confront her before she knows more. They're busy sorting out things so you're going to be okay. I guess I'll have to deal with what's to come too…"

Max turns abruptly and starts walking. Ella feels like her shoes are made of lead as she follows Max up the stairs.

Chapter 14

Mᴀx ʜᴏʟᴅs ᴀ ᴅᴏᴏʀ ᴏᴘᴇɴ, and beyond it, Ella finds the room packed with men and women, some of whom she recognises from the second night's investor meeting. She also sees her step-mother and step-sisters sitting at the table, and all three glare her with seething anger.

"Ah, I see you found my son."

"Your son?" Ella asks hesitantly.
"My name is Max Burley." Max's voice sounds devoid of emotion.

"Ha! And you probably thought you had snagged him."

Ella stares her oldest step-sister angrily, "Snagged him." Ella mouths. "What does she mean?"
"I guess my son kept to *his* side of the bargain and made sure no one was told who he *really* is. Ella, I cannot wave a magic wand like I'm some sort of Fairy Godmother, but I can make sure *they* don't ever bother you. But to do that I needed evidence."
"I'm an undercover cop, Ella. I came here to do a job because my father asked me. What I didn't count on is to

fall in love with you in the process."

"You're a cop?"

"Yes."

"Hmmm, that explains it."

"Explains what?" Max frowns, looking confused.

"All the questions you kept asking. I guess you needed specific details to confirm what your father suspected."

"Roger Chase was one of my closest friends. When he died, seemingly in perfect health, and then somehow you disappeared off the face of the earth a few weeks later I knew something was wrong. *Her* changing the deeds of your house, changing the name of the company that I once helped to start with a sizable investment, and—"

"What you do you mean about me disappearing?"

"Don't you know?" Max reaches into a pocket in his jacket and pulls out a piece of paper. "Remember a few days ago when I asked you what your full name is…"

Ella nods, and hesitantly accepts the paper Max is holding out. She glances at it and her face contorts into anger and disgust. She glares at her step-mother before she yells, "Did you try to claim that somehow I decided to jump off a bridge, you evil disgusting bitch?"

Ella is met by laughter. From all three individuals sitting at the table, all sneering at her once more before laughing even more. Ella starts to walk towards them, but she's stopped.

"They're not worth it. They'll go to court and then go to jail for a very long time." Max says softly.

Ella glances up at Max, "Can you promise that?"

"Yes. All these people here are my friends, Ella. They, and I, and Max as well, we'll all testify against them. What we're doing *now* won't bring back your father, but what we do *now* can give you a new and better life."

"I'd like to be part of that life, if you'll have me, Ella." Max whispers. "I love you. I guess I fell in love with you when we started talking that night when you were sitting in the chair that was over there…"

Max nods, and Ella glances over her shoulder. He nodded towards where the exquisitely grandiose leather chair was located when he'd made his presence known to her.

Ella looks up at Max. He flashes a weak smile at her before he speaks again, "If you'll have me…"

It only takes a moment of hesitation before Ella's arms find themselves around his neck, and before she finds herself kissing him. She feels his arms slide around her waist and feels herself suddenly being pulled even closer.

Ella only partially hears the protests coming from her step-mother and step-sisters, "Ellaaaa, we can be friends, can't we? Take your filthy hands off me. Ellaaa, please, listen to me. It was mother who did this, not us. We're innocent. We never meant any of it."

Minutes later the room is silent again. Ella feels a soft tap on her shoulder, "Ella, you need to sign a few pieces of paperwork."

Ella looks perplexed at tall man standing beside her.

"After signing it, all this will be all yours. Like your father wanted."

"Only on *one* condition…" Ella states softly.

"What condition?"

"That you *stop* bugging Max about his choice of career. I love him just the way he *is,* and before he started this business Dad was a cop *too.*"

"I guess I can live with that condition."

"Me too." Max adds.

"I have a condition for you too, Max."

"Oh, oh."

"I want you to teach me everything you know so I can continue with my dad's legacy. When I saw the cleaning machine that night, I realised that I should be doing what he did while he lived. I want this company to thrive, and I'm going to need help for it."

"So, I guess I'll do my cop work part time…"

"Only if you want to. One thing I've learnt from all this, is that forcing people into something they don't want to do, isn't helpful for anyone."

"I guess I can do that, but I have one condition as well."

"What condition?"

"That you forgive me for deceiving you all this time. I couldn't tell you. Honestly."

"I guess I can forgive my very own Prince Charming."

"I guess I'll be Prince Charming if you'll be my future Mrs Burley…"

"You come here for three months of undercover work and end up falling in love in the process."

"Yes, father, that happened. But as I said to Ella. It's up to her, and I hope she forgives me for deceiving her…"

"There's nothing to forgive. All I remember is a *kind* man who took pity on a damsel in distress, helped her cope, and then helped to *leave* from here. I love you *too*, Max Burley."

"I guess there's a wedding on the cards."

"Yes, father, that's precisely what's going to happen. But *only* when Ellana Chase tells *me* she wants it. I think this is her *last* day of someone dictating to *her* how to live her life…"

THE END

www.ingramcontent.com/pod-product-compliance
Lightning Source LLC
LaVergne TN
LVHW021241200726
843509LV00012B/1561